VIKING
Published by the Penguin Group
Penguin Books USA Inc., 375 Hudson Street, New York, New York 10014, U.S.A.
Penguin Books Ltd, 27 Wrights Lane, London W8 5TZ, England
Penguin Books Australia Ltd, Ringwood, Victoria, Australia
Penguin Books Canada Ltd, 10 Alcorn Avenue, Toronto, Ontario, Canada M4V 3B2
Penguin Books (N.Z.) Ltd, 182-190 Wairau Road, Auckland 10, New Zealand

Penguin Books Ltd, Registered Offices: Harmondsworth, Middlesex, England

First published in 1995 by Viking, a division of Penguin Books USA Inc.

10 9 8 7 6 5 4 3

LIBRARY OF CONGRESS CATALOGING-IN-PUBLICATION DATA
Seibold, J. Otto.
Monkey business / by J. Otto Seibold and Vivian Walsh.   p.   cm.
Summary : Space Monkey, an ex-astronaut turned monkey tycoon, discovers that his
company's one millionth product has been inhabited by a bug named Penelope.
ISBN 0-670-86393-9 (hardcover)
[1. Monkeys—Fiction. 2. Business enterprises—Fiction. 3. Insects—Fiction.]
I. Walsh, Vivian. II. Title.
PZ7.S45513Mm 1995
[E]—dc20   95-4577 CIP AC

Printed in Hong Kong
Set in Futura and featuring Manu Sans and Cyberotica

The illustrations in this book were created on an Apple Macintosh computer
using Adobe Illustrator software.

MONKEY BUSINESS

(le concerne du primate)

A LONG TIME AGO

a monkey was shot into space —in a rocket ship! His name was Space Monkey. At the time rocket ships were not safe enough for people, so a brave volunteer was needed for the dangerous ride. Space Monkey came forward, and after some training he was ready to go.

His rocket ship circled the earth twice and then landed in the ocean. A helicopter was sent to pick him up, and he was given a ticker-tape parade—the first for a monkey.

His mission was a success, and he retired from the space program. The people of Earth (our planet) were so thankful for Space Monkey's bravery that they gave him his own company. He called it MONKEY BUSINESS.

Space Monkey went right to work. Using a super-computer, a gift from his friends at the space program, he accidentally made something brand new. It looked like something he'd seen floating in space. Although he wasn't sure what it was, it turned out to be tremendously popular.

People wanted so many of them that soon the Monkey Business factory would finish its millionth one.

THIS IS WHAT HE MADE.

Space Monkey often dreamed about the millionth product. He had big plans for it. It was to be the star attraction in the Monkey Business Museum (located in the building's lobby). A glass case would house the museum's new centerpiece.

Space Monkey wished the assembly line could go faster, but he also believed in factory safety.

It takes a long time to get to a million. While Space Monkey was waiting, he fell asleep.

As Space Monkey slept, one of his trucks was making a delivery on the other side of town. The truck driver was so busy with the road that he almost didn't notice a tiny bug in the crosswalk.

The driver swerved and ended up hitting his head on a lamppost. That kept him from noticing that something had fallen off the back of the truck and landed in front of the bug, whose name was Penelope.

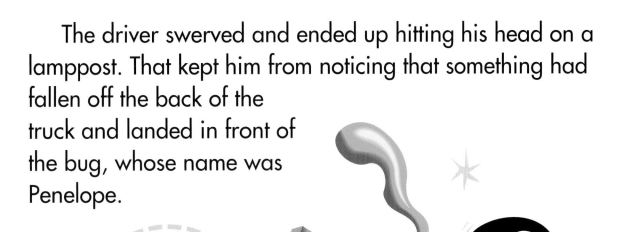

Penelope flew straight up to get a better look. "What's this?" she wondered.

Whatever it was, it was too heavy for Penelope to lift, so she sat down to admire it.

After a while, a man came along pulling a wagon. Penelope watched as he put the mysterious object in his wagon and turned around to go home. She followed him.

The man wasn't sure what he had found, but he liked the way it looked on top of his television set. He was making sure it looked good from his chair when he heard a suspiciously buglike buzz. He grabbed a flyswatter and spun around to face the intruder. Penelope quickly introduced herself and began to explain what she was doing in his house.

Penelope began to explain...

She told the sad story of how she had lost her home that morning. A bird stepped on it. She escaped just in time, but her house was smashed. After the smoke had cleared she remembered the wise words of her mother: "When a bird steps on your house, find another."

She had been searching for hours, when something fell from the sky and landed at her feet. She knew then that her luck had changed.

The man was touched by Penelope's story. He dropped the swatter and introduced himself. "My name is Quincy," he said.

Quincy invited Penelope to watch TV with him. He aimed the remote control and pressed the button, but the beam missed the television and hit the new decoration instead.

All at once a bright light and some friendly music filled the room. The mysterious object shuddered, and slowly a door began to open.

Quincy was surprised. Penelope was amazed. After the music stopped and the room returned to normal they went to have a closer look. Penelope knew that she was the one who must go through the door—it was just her size.

Inside, she found a room that looked as if it had been made just for her. It had a little bed, a little chair, a little drinking glass, and a tiny vase with a flower in it. Penelope lay down on the bed. It felt so nice that she let out a little bug sigh.

She was very happy. She had found a new home.

Meanwhile, back at Monkey Business, the supercomputer was going over a few calculations.

An alarm went off in the computer's head. It had to wake up Space Monkey to tell him some very bad news. It had miscalculated! The millionth product had been made—and was lost!

It had disappeared when a Monkey Business truck crashed into a lamppost.

Space Monkey was worried. He had to think of something fast.

He decided to use his fame as a monkey astronaut and go on television to make a nationwide plea for the return of his missing millionth product.

The important news flash made it all the way to the television set just below Penelope's new home.

She realized right away that her new home was also Space Monkey's missing millionth product. Then she realized she and Quincy would have to return it to him.

They didn't waste any time. Using extra care, they tied the object to the top of Quincy's automobile. Then they sped off to find the Monkey Business headquarters.

When Space Monkey saw they had his millionth product he became very excited. The computer calculated that there was a good chance the two were troublemakers. Space Monkey said there was no need to worry —he had a plan.

"Hello!" he called. "How do you do. Please come in." Although he spoke kindly, he was secretly opening a drawer with his tail. He smiled at his guests as his tail hit the emergency CAPTURE  button. That was the computer's signal. It leaped out and dropped a glass cage over the little pink bug.

First a bird had wrecked Penelope's house, then Quincy frightened her with a flyswatter, and now Space Monkey had her in a trap.

"Why is everybody being so mean?" thought Penelope.

"There is no need for cages," said Quincy. "We didn't take anything of yours. We found something." Using the remote control, Quincy made the little door open again. Space Monkey looked inside and saw the tiny, bug-sized room. He'd always wondered what was in those things.

Space Monkey thought it was best to change the subject. He complimented Penelope on her flying, adding that he himself had enjoyed floating in zero gravity.

Penelope said that with some tutoring he could probably learn to fly again. They agreed that in exchange for flying lessons Space Monkey would give Penelope the little bug house.

The Monkey Business Museum would have to wait for number one billion.

After some practice
Space Monkey became
a pretty good flyer.